Thank You
Modeh Ani

By Rabbi Alyson Solomon

Illustrated by Bryony Clarkson

APPLES & HONEY PRESS

Thank You: Modeh Ani is dedicated to and inspired by my parents, Stephen Lee, z"l, and Susan Mae, who woke me with wonder and tucked me in with love. —RAS

For Finn, Scarlett, and Madeleine —BC

Modeh ani means "I am grateful" in Hebrew. *Thank You: Modeh Ani* is inspired by Jewish prayers of gratitude for waking up to a new day.

The illustrations for this book were created using a combination of cut-paper collage, acrylic and watercolor paint, and colored pencil. The original artwork is scanned and lightly enhanced with digital processing to complete the illustration.

Apples & Honey Press
An Imprint of Behrman House Publishers
Millburn, New Jersey 07041
www.applesandhoneypress.com

ISBN 978-1-68115-569-2

Text copyright © 2021 by Rabbi Alyson Solomon
Illustrations copyright © 2021 by Behrman House

Library of Congress Cataloging-in-Publication Data
Names: Solomon, Alyson, author. | Clarkson, Bryony, illustrator.
Title: Thank You: Modeh Ani / by Alyson Solomon ; illustrated by Bryony
  Clarkson.
Description: Millburn : Apples and Honey Press, 2021. | Audience: Grades
  K-1 | Summary: Modeh Ani means "I am grateful" in Hebrew and is inspired
  by Jewish prayers of gratitude for waking up to a new day. In this book
  children dance, jump and sing their gratitude.
Identifiers: LCCN 2020031981 | ISBN 9781681155692 (hardcover)
Subjects: LCSH: Morning benedictions—Adaptations—Juvenile literature.
Classification: LCC BM670.M67 S65 2021 | DDC 296.4/5—dc23
LC record available at https://lccn.loc.gov/2020031981

Design by Anne Redmond
Edited by Dena Neusner
Art direction by Ann D. Koffsky
Printed in China

10 9 8 7 6 5 4 3 2 1

0222/B1846/A3

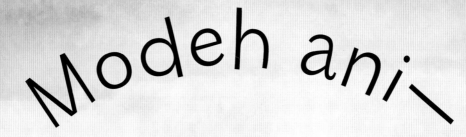

Modeh ani~

Thank You for this brand-new day.
My whole body is grateful.

Thank You for my toes that tap,

my feet that point.

Thank You for
my ankles that 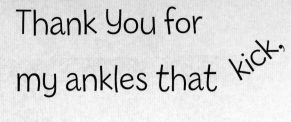 kick,

my knees that bend.

Thank You for

my hips that dance,

my waist that wiggles.

Modeh ani

Thank You for
this new day.

Thank You for

my breath that goes in and out,
my heart that beats fast and s l o w.

Thank You for
my bones that
grow strong.
My branches reach high,
my roots dig deep.

Thank You for
my fingers that wave,
my hands that hold,
my elbows that bend,

my shoulders that shimmy.

Thank You for

my muscles that s t r e t c h,

my neck that holds my head up high.

Thank You for
my face with all its doors:
my eyes that squint,
my ears that hear,
my nose that sniffs,

my mouth that

sings out songs and prayers.

My whole body is
ready for this
bright new day.

Thank You —
Modeh Ani!

Dear Families,

Modeh ani means "thank you" or "I am grateful" in Hebrew. What are you grateful for? How does it feel, inside your body, when you are grateful?

This book is inspired by two Jewish prayers that are said in the morning upon waking: Modeh Ani and Asher Yatzar.

Modeh Ani starts with "I am grateful to You." This prayer thanks God for waking us to start the day fresh, and to enjoy the world through our bodies that move and groove. As a proud woman, I sing out *Mod**ah** ani*, the feminine form. You might make up your own words of "Wow, thanks!" or "Go, God!" or "Yay, a new day!" You can choose how you want to say it. Maybe even mix it up, sing it, or shout it out!

Asher yatzar means "who forms." This prayer thanks God for forming our bodies in the intricate ways that they open and close, heal, and move. (This prayer is said after we go to the bathroom—yes, Jewish tradition has a blessing for everything!) In this book, we start with our toes and move toward our noses, aware of our bodies, the ground beneath us, this very moment that we are alive.

I hope this book inspires your family to start each day ready to move, to dance, to wiggle, and to sing. What will you say *modeh ani* for today?

Wishing you a joyful day,

Rabbi Alyson Solomon